This edition first published in 2014
by Book Island, Raumati South, New Zealand
info@bookisland.co.nz

Text © Fundacja im. Juliana Tuwima i Ireny Tuwim 2006
Illustrations © Bohdan Butenko 1956
English language translation © Antonia Lloyd-Jones 2014
English language edition © Book Island 2014

Original title: Pan Maluśkiewicz i Wieloryb
© Wydawnictwo Dwie Siostry Warsaw 2008

A catalogue record for this book is available from the National Library of New Zealand.

Edited by Frith Williams
Typeset by Vida & Luke Kelly, New Zealand

Printed by Everbest, China

The publication of this book has been made possible with the
financial support of the Polish Translation Programme of the
Polish Book Institute.

ISBN Hardback: 978-0-9876696-8-1
ISBN Paperback: 978-0-9876696-9-8

Visit www.bookisland.co.nz for more information about our titles.

MR MINISCULE AND THE
WHALE

BOOK ISLAND

Julian Tuwim

MR MINISCULE AND THE
WHALE

Illustrated by
BOHDAN BUTENKO

Translated by
ANTONIA LLOYD-JONES

BOOK ISLAND

A man called Mr Miniscule
is the hero of this tale.
Far he'd been and much he'd seen
except for a big blue whale.

Mr Miniscule was half the height
of a coffee bean, no more,
but still he loved to travel,
but still he loved to explore.

Indeed it's really no surprise
that he longed to see a whale,
for a whale is as big as a sailing ship
from its head to the tip of its tail.

Mr Miniscule could barely wait
to get himself afloat,
and so, from half a walnut shell,
he built himself a boat.

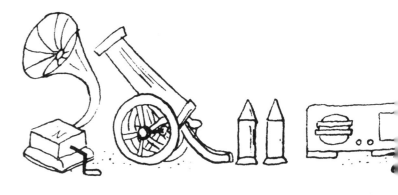

And to make it nice and cosy,
he laid cotton wool on the floor,
then used a single wooden match
to whittle himself four oars.

He took a sack he'd filled with food,
a barrel of wine and a tent,
all sorts of tools and a bicycle –
into the boat they went.

A radio, a cannon, a gramophone,
a rifle and bullets he stored,
a fur coat, slippers, and underwear,
he took the lot on board.

For all his things were tiny,
teeny-weeny, very small,
like Mr Miniscule himself
they took no space at all.

With his vessel finally ready,
he boarded a butterfly plane
and off he flew to the seashore,
then fluttered down again.

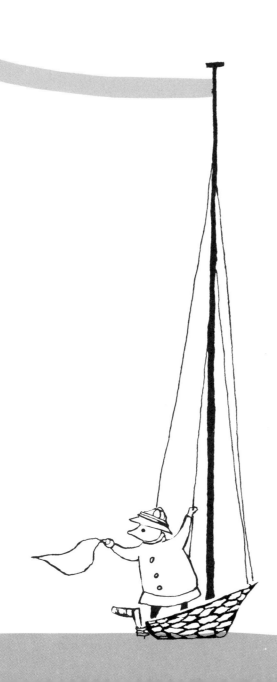

At the port he conferred with the captain
of a giant ocean cruiser.
'Is there space on the sea for one more?'
'Aye, *plenty of room for you, sir!*'

So tiny Mr Miniscule
cast off without delay.
He sailed and sailed and never stopped,
further and further away.

The sea was as quiet and calm and clear
as the water in a pail,
but even so he couldn't see
the faintest sign of a whale.

At first he rowed with one of his oars,
then two, then three, then four.
For two weeks he was sailing,
but never a whale he saw.

He called out, 'Here boy, Mister Whale,
where *are* you, my fishy friend?
Show me just a hint of your head
or a flash of your tail end.'

For two months he was sailing,
but never a whale he saw.
Poor fellow, he was tired now
and dozing more and more.

Oh what a luxurious sleep he'd have
on a bed of golden sand ...
then one day he looked out to sea
and ahead he sighted land.

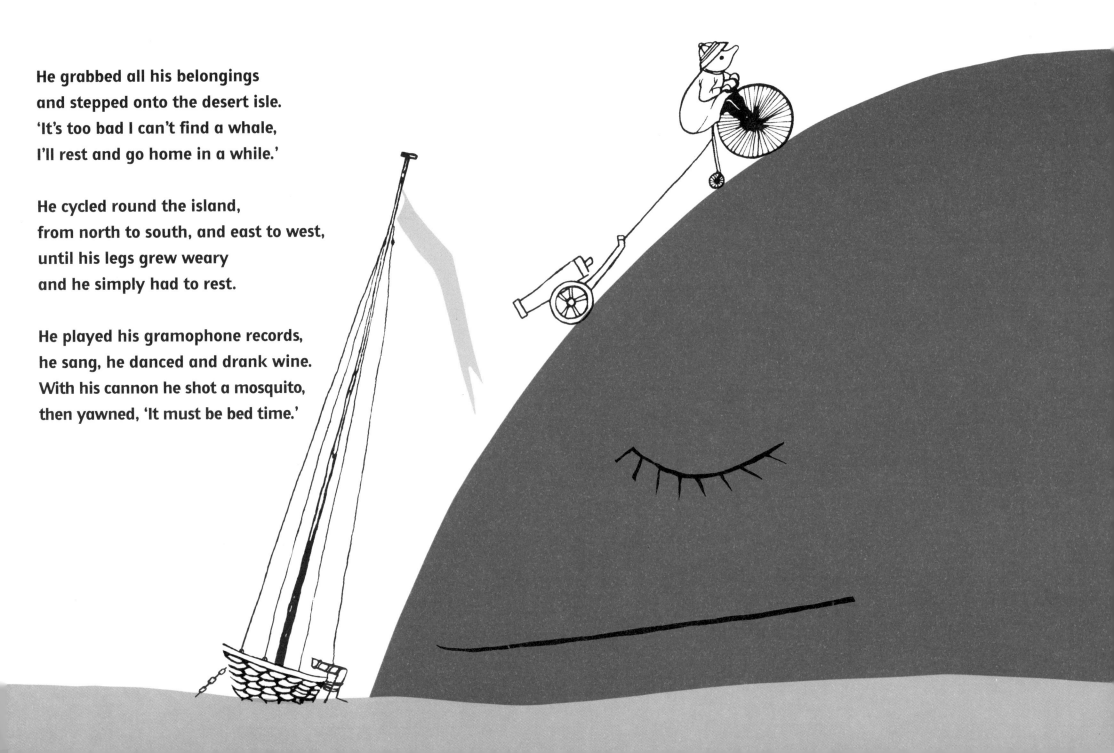

He grabbed all his belongings
and stepped onto the desert isle.
'It's too bad I can't find a whale,
I'll rest and go home in a while.'

He cycled round the island,
from north to south, and east to west,
until his legs grew weary
and he simply had to rest.

He played his gramophone records,
he sang, he danced and drank wine.
With his cannon he shot a mosquito,
then yawned, 'It must be bed time.'

With his tiny tent in hand,
he knelt down on one knee
and began to bang the pegs in ...
when the island suddenly sneezed!

It sneezed and gave a mighty roar:
'Now what's all this about?
What silly fool would pitch his tent
atop a whale's spout?'

'A wh-wh-whale?' stammered Miniscule,
trying hard to stay composed.
'*Can't you see, you nincompoop,
you've hit me on the nose!*

*My belly's underwater.
Be glad you're still intact.*'
'But isn't this an island ...?'
'*No, you're standing on my back!*'

Mr Miniscule was trembling.
'Do stop that tickling, sir!'
'I'm not t-t-tickling, Mr Whale,
I think it's time I went – adieu.'

He grabbed all his belongings,
and rushed off to his boat,
then headed back to harbour
as fast as he could float.

And now if anyone stops to ask
if he's ever seen a whale,
he says, with nose up in the air,
'More than just its tail!'

Julian Tuwim (1894–1953) was one of Poland's leading poets. He won fame not just for his adult verse but also for his rhymes for children, many of which are classics known to every Polish child. He also wrote satirical verse and loved word games, inventing palindromes (whole sentences that read the same forwards and backwards), lipograms (whole paragraphs that leave out a particular letter), and tautograms (sentences where every word starts with the same letter). Nobody knows if he ever set out to sea to see a whale.

Bohdan Butenko (born 1931) is one of Poland's top illustrators, whose drawings appear in more than 200 children's books. He is also famous for his animated cartoons – especially featuring Gucio the clumsy hippo and Cezar the sensible dog – as well as for his stage sets and television design. He has won many prizes, among them the 2012 Order of the Smile – a special medal awarded by children to adults who are particularly kind to them.